Humphrey and the Seven Golden Rings

J. B. Heart

Cool Breeze
WRITERS & PUBLISHERS

Humphrey and the Seven Golden Rings

by J.B. Heart

Copyright © 2014 J.B. Heart

Published by Cool Breeze Writers and Publishers
www.CoolBreezePublishing.com

Paperback: ISBN # 978-0-9915741-1-7

Illustrations, cover and interior design by Kathryn Marcellino

Printed in the United States of America

Table of Contents

Chapter One

Humphrey was born much like any other caterpillar; small, frail and clear. His parents, king and queen of the butterflies, would say to their friends, "Look at our boy, he's so healthy, he's so handsome." His parents would say it so often that Humphrey's brothers soon got jealous. They began to lie to Humphrey. He was so young and trusting, he began to believe these lies.

When they told him he was worthless, he believed them.

When they told him he was ugly, he believed them.

When they told him he was weak, he believed them.

When they told him he would never be loved, he believed them.

When they told him he would never amount to anything, he believed them.

When they told him he was the most hated caterpillar alive, he believed them.

When they told him that he wasn't really their brother, he believed them.

The lies continued and grew worse and worse, until one day Humphrey, believing his brothers' lies, ran away from home. He crawled deep into the forest, where his brothers told him he was really from.

Humphrey traveled for weeks, journeying through the forest, seeing things that filled him with awe. From birds, with their beautiful song, to strange, hard creatures with large claws, wandering along the ground, that snapped at things as they approached.

In search of his real parents, Humphrey came across a magic glade hidden deep in the woods. It was filled with glowing lights that floated softly in the air, bobbing as though they were in water. Darting around like fairies, the lights slowly bounced toward Humphrey, and he felt calm for the first time in his travels. All around him the trees glowed a soft and beautiful shade of green and white, filling his heart with comfort. Rubbing his eyes in disbelief, he looked around and, not aware of the magic that he'd found, Humphrey tried and tried, but could find no way out of the glade.

As he walked around, he grew hungry. Looking up in the trees, he saw that their leaves looked absolutely delicious. Soon he began eating leaves from the magical trees. The leaves were the best thing he'd ever tasted, and he soon began to eat more and more, until he felt so full, he thought he might explode.

"Oh, my belly hurts," Humphrey said, as he tried to find a safe place to settle down to rest his body. As he began to make himself a bed with his silk, his belly began to hurt even more. Then, before his very eyes, it began to snow in the glade. Within moments, Humphrey grew frightfully cold, so he spun his silk around him to keep himself warmer through the night.

As Humphrey slept in his tight, warm cocoon, he dreamt of the castle he'd left, and all its glory and splendor. Massive white silken walls held within them long halls of polished stone that you could see yourself on. Immense meals of the most select leaves and nectars graced the tables of the royal family. Despite being so full, Humphrey dreamt that he was growing hungry again. Reaching for an almost impossibly beautiful cupful of the most fragrant nectar he'd ever seen, Humphrey felt his hand pulled away from the table, and his eldest brother said, "This meal is only for true members of the royal family, not for commoner trash like you, Humphrey."

Still dreaming, Humphrey's youngest brother stepped beside him and pulled his chair out so fast that Humphrey fell to the floor. He heard his brothers say in unison, with cruelty and laughter tainting their almost-musical voices: "You're not even fit to know our names!"

As he lay upon the floor, Humphrey began to cry. His seven brothers began to chant: "Bow to us. Bow to us. Bow to us."

Humphrey awoke with a jump, his eyes filled with tears and his cheeks covered in sweat, despite the cold he'd escaped. Looking around, he saw that he was still wrapped in his cocoon, and began to tear at it to get out.

As he tore through the cocoon, eating parts of it, he was shocked to see that it tasted as good as the leaves he'd eaten before he fell asleep. He broke free of his cocoon and reached for leaves nearby, and used them to make a small pouch. He stored the rest of his cocoon, more than half his body length, in it. Surprised it had fit, Humphrey reached inside and was shocked to find that there was still quite a bit of room within.

Humming happily to himself, things going well for the first time in quite a while, Humphrey made his way to the ground. He was so focused on his goal that he barely noticed that the glade was much warmer now, as though he'd gone to sleep in summer, and hadn't been escaping snow. For a brief moment he grew concerned, as he noticed he was moving a bit slower than he had before he'd gone to sleep.

Reaching the ground, Humphrey caught sight of himself in a puddle of water and, shocked at what he'd thought he'd seen, he examined himself closer in the puddle. Humphrey, previously clear and frail, was now a pure, beaming white. Looking along his body in his reflection more, he saw that there were now seven golden rings at various points from the end of his body all the way up to his neck, just beneath his head. Curious about the rings, Humphrey put the matter out of his mind and set about looking for a way out again.

As he wandered through the glade, Humphrey came across a strange stick, sticking out of a stone in the middle of the clearing. Despite being a fragile, ugly little stick, it had clearly been stabbed clear through the stone, not even cracking on the way through. As he looked at it, the stick began to remind Humphrey of how he felt about himself; weak, unwanted and discarded. It would make an excellent companion on his journey.

Reaching for the stick, Humphrey said, "Come along, little friend. We'll keep each other company."

Pulling at the stick, it flew from the stone as though it had been resting in water instead being embedded in solid rock. Smiling at his good fortune, Humphrey attempted to put the stick in his pouch, and was pleasantly surprised to find that not only did it fit within, but he also had an exceptional amount of space remaining in his pouch.

Walking to a nearby tree, he set about making several leaf containers for nectar, and also gathered quite a few leaves to eat as he searched for his family.

He began filling his pack and tried to fill it to the brim, but no matter how many leaves or containers of nectar he placed in the pack, it never so much as grew heavy, let alone ran out of space. In fact, he soon found that whenever he reached into the pack, he pulled out exactly what he'd been seeking. Smiling happily at this discovery, Humphrey spent the rest of the day eating, and filling the pack.

Climbing a tree, he prepared to make himself another cocoon for warmth when he heard a small voice. Looking around, he saw one of the strange creatures from his previous travels along the ground.

"Please help me," the voice cried, panicked.

Climbing down the tree as fast as he could, Humphrey saw this strange creature being attacked by large, black ants. The ants howled war chants at the creature as they attacked it and called it the "Living Stone."

Reaching for his stick, Humphrey began swinging at the ants, and quickly drove them away from the creature. The ants glared at Humphrey as they ran from him, and vowed revenge.

Sighing in relief, the creature looked at Humphrey and said, "Thank you so much for your help! I can't possibly thank you enough Mr...."

Catching the creature's drift, Humphrey smiled and said, "My name's Humphrey. What's your name? And please don't think I'm rude, but what are you?"

Laughing quietly, the creature spoke calmly, "My name is Adam. I'm a blue crab from the ocean."

"What's a crab?" Humphrey asked curiously.

Laughing louder now, Adam said, "I'm a sea creature. My people are seeking wealth here in the forest, and I was interested in this strange little puddle here. It glowed so beautifully from afar, like liquid diamonds. I admit, my greed overcame me and when I approached it, my heart was shrouded with avarice. When I placed my claw into it, seeking to take it for my own, those ants attacked me."

Humphrey nodded and said, "Yeah, ants can be violent if you cross their territory or take their treasures."

Adam reached onto his back, where a small pack had been strapped. He pulled out a small whistle and handed it to Humphrey, saying, "If you ever need help, blow this, and we will come to your assistance."

The whistle was a simple thing, made out of a material Humphrey had never seen before. He assumed it had come from the sea.

Humphrey looked at the crab curiously and said, "We?"

Adam nodded and said cryptically, "We are legion."

Turning without explaining his curious statement, Adam walked toward and through a tree as though it weren't even there.

Running as fast as he could, Humphrey soon realized that the tree wasn't really there and smiled happily, climbing a nearby tree to prepare for sleep as it began to snow again within the glade.

After he was finished wrapping himself in his cocoon, Humphrey laid his head down and drifted off to sleep.

His dreams, while no less upsetting than the night before, were shorter this night. His brothers all came and stopped him from eating, but while he was on the floor crying this night, his youngest brother, Able, came and tried to comfort him.

Waking again with a shock, Humphrey repeated the process of breaking out and eating part of his cocoon, again noting that it tasted delicious, perhaps even more delicious than it had the first time. Putting the rest of his cocoon into his pack, he climbed, even slower now, down the tree. He found that he was larger now than he had been the day before, and that he was an even purer shade of white than before. The six golden rings on his body practically shone with their brilliance, and he began walking out of the glade. As he walked, he mumbled to himself, "Weren't there seven rings yesterday?"

Chapter Two

Leaving the glade, Humphrey felt refreshed and calm, a sensation he'd never felt before. Walking forward, his mind clear and his body stronger, he soon found himself resting. The moon began to rise, full and beautiful. He hadn't even noticed the day go by and it was already evening. He wondered how far he'd gone. Looking around for some kind of landmark, he noticed a small village of caterpillars and other creatures nearby, and began to move toward them.

As he walked, he heard several feminine voices giggling around him. Soon he found himself blushing in shyness. The giggling continued, unseen, until he reached a small inn near the outskirts of the town.

Stepping inside, Humphrey received shocked looks from all around the inn. He did his best to ignore the onlookers. All of the caterpillars around him had long hair, slicked back as though they'd just come out of the water. Walking to the counter where the innkeeper stood, his mouth agape, Humphrey asked, "Is there something strange about me?"

The innkeeper didn't respond. His mouth was still open, and Humphrey tried to get his attention with a joke. "If you keep your mouth open like that, you'll catch flies and put the local dragonflies to shame."

The innkeeper shook his head a bit and said, "If you're looking for a room here, you won't be able to get one…"

Frowning a bit, Humphrey asked, "Is there something wrong with me that makes me unable to get a room here? Am I too ugly for this inn? If so, I can leave…"

So accustomed to his brothers' lies, Humphrey had taken to avoiding other caterpillars on his trip thus far and had forgotten, for a time, that he was as hideous as he was.

The innkeeper began to speak when Humphrey cut him off and said, "It's okay…I wouldn't want a plain caterpillar like me here either. If you have a closet away from the others, I'll stay there if you'd like."

The innkeeper spoke up. "Nonsense! You may be a little bigger than the rest of us…but I refuse to let you stay anywhere but in the loft, where you'll be safe."

Thinking the innkeeper was referencing other caterpillars who would want to harm him, Humphrey was extremely grateful and asked, "What would you like in return?"

Caterpillars, being mostly a food and beauty-based society, rarely exchanged any form of currency, relying mostly on bartering, or trading services.

The innkeeper shook his head and said, "Nothing. You'll stay in the loft for free…please…make yourself comfortable, and eat as much as you'd like."

Humphrey nodded a thank you and shuffled toward the stairs. Fearing that he'd be poisoned, he thought to himself, "I'll eat from my reserves…just to be safe."

Climbing the stairs, he overheard the innkeeper saying, his voice harsh and angry, "You leave him alone. Your kind has no right to even approach him."

Thinking the innkeeper was talking to him, a tear fell from Humphrey's eyes. His nightmares of his brothers coming to mind, he set his eyes on the stairs ahead of him and walked as fast as he could.

Reaching the loft, Humphrey set his pack in the center of the room, bare except for a small closet in the far corner. He pulled out several leaves, somehow still fresh and near full-size, almost as big as Humphrey himself. Wondering at his bag in silence, Humphrey began to eat and drink from a nectar container that he pulled from the bag from time to time. The incredible taste of the leaves and nectar filled him with happiness, wiping doubt and sadness from his mind for a moment. He soon began to craft his cocoon for the night.

In his dreams, filled with hateful voices, Humphrey found himself on a cliff top overlooking the whole of the forest, in all its glory. The voices shouted their normal cacophony, but this time he ignored them, and dove into the forest below. It bent around him like water, splashing outward and away, while the liquid forest engulfed him in what he could only imagine, from its taste, was the nectar from the glade.

As he fell through the nectar, his brothers' faces began to appear, all six of the voices from the previous night glaring at him with violent hatred. Only Able's face appeared loving.

Awakening from his dream and trying to take solace in Able's loving countenance, Humphrey broke out of his cocoon, not hungry in the slightest. He suspected, since his head now touched the ceiling, that he had grown bigger.

Wrapping his cocoon up and putting it into his bag, Humphrey began his trek down the stairs, ducking his head through the door.

"My, you're fat," a girl's voice shouted out, mocking him with her lilt and laughter.

The innkeeper's voice shouted loudly, "Esmeralda! Enough of your nonsense! Let our visitor depart in peace!"

Running over to Humphrey and touching his side, the young, black-haired caterpillar said loudly, "I can't imagine how you even got in at this size." She ran her fingers along the rings on Humphrey's body and said, "Not only are you big, you're a gaudy fellow too, eh? Five golden rings tattooed onto your body. Feeling confident?"

"Five?" Humphrey asked, as he looked at the young girl and was shocked at her beauty. She was possibly the most beautiful caterpillar maiden he'd ever seen in his life.

The girl, Esmeralda whipped her hair behind her and nodded as she said, "Who are you, anyway?"

Humphrey smiled and said calmly, "I'm Humphrey, Ms. Esmeralda."

The innkeeper frowned and said to Humphrey, "I'm terribly sorry for my daughter's behavior. Please, if it would please you, stay for as long as you'd like."

Humphrey's thoughts went to the parents he was seeking, and he figured to himself that he would make do in the town he was in. There was no way to know who his real parents were, let alone find them.

"Is there anything I could do to rent out the loft, full-time?" Humphrey asked the innkeeper.

Smiling gently and nodding his head, the innkeeper said, "It is yours."

Taken aback by the innkeeper's generosity, Humphrey spoke quietly and thankfully and said, "Thank you so much. I can never repay you for this."

The innkeeper, older and wiser than Humphrey said, "The golden rings on your body, do you know why they glow so?"

Shaking his head, Humphrey said, "I honestly didn't realize they glowed so brightly."

Smiling and laughing, the innkeeper said, "They glow brightly, like suns trapped in the dew in the early morning light. They glow because you shine with inner glory, a gift from above, if ever I have seen one."

Esmeralda said in a dark voice, "Yeah, you distracted all the men here last night from me, and it was very difficult to talk to anyone."

"I'd thought it was that my appearance was horrific," Humphrey said quietly.

Esmeralda jumped back in surprise and said, "You are massive, I will give you that. But horrific, you are not. You are rather handsome, in my opinion."

Looking at the girl and seeing her beauty even clearer now, he bowed his head in thanks and began to walk toward the stairs, his head held high in pride.

Within his cocoon, he dreamt of spider silk soup and aphid nectar tea. His youngest brother, Able, and his second youngest and strongest brother, Marcus, were eating alongside him, while his five remaining brothers scowled from the shadows of the doorway, hating him from afar.

Chapter Three

Weeks passed in this manner, and soon Humphrey took a position watching the front desk, which was heavily modified to accommodate his large size. As the days flew by, he and Esmeralda grew closer, though she kept insisting that his size would forever doom him to never be with her.

Ignoring her statements about his size, he never felt the weight of his appearance again, he never felt hideous or unwanted. The rest of the town soon began to come by to talk to the well-traveled caterpillar about his experiences and what he'd seen, though he never mentioned the softly glowing glade or the special traits of his ever-roomy pack. He knew that they'd just think he was crazy. He figured that no matter how much he was liked, the pack would only inspire dangerous greed against him.

One day, as he was sleeping in his cocoon, he heard a skittering sound. There was a rapid tapping of feet along the ground and then a scream pierced the night, shocking him into alert wakefulness.

Humphrey ran as fast as he could (not very fast as he'd grown larger since first coming to the town). Humphrey found a note that said, "The fat caterpillar has insulted our king and unless he is brought to us, dead, the girl will die in his place to sate our rage."

The innkeeper, his heart broken by the kidnapping of his daughter, turned to Humphrey and said, "The ants have always been cruel to our people, my friend...I cannot ask this of you...but please...save my daughter, if you can."

Humphrey had never lied to his fellow caterpillars, or the myriad other people in the town, but they believed he could save Esmeralda, despite his honest lack of combat experience.

Thinking to himself, he whispered aloud, "I will try." Retreating to his loft, he formed the largest cocoon he'd ever made, where he stayed for days and days, searching desperately for a plan to save the woman he loved.

As he slumbered, the idea finally struck him, so hard that he simply cut his way out of his cocoon in excitement. Leaving the cocoon in shambles on the floor of his room, he raced down the stairs and shouted to the innkeeper, "I have an idea!"

The innkeeper stared at Humphrey for a long time before he said, "Humphrey?"

Rolling his eyes, Humphrey said, "Yes, yes, I'm probably bigger...but I know how to save Esmeralda!"

Shaking his head, the innkeeper turned a polished stone toward Humphrey and said, "You're not bigger, Humphrey..."

Getting annoyed, Humphrey looked at the stone, polished to a near-perfect reflective gloss, and saw what could only be described as incredible.

He'd changed form in the days he spent in the cocoon. His large body had been replaced with a thin form. His body was black like ink, but the wings he'd grown were the same glowing white as his body had been, with four glowing golden rings, one at each tip of his wings. At rest, they hung like a cloak about his body; but when he moved them, they sprung to glorious action, so fast that they could barely be followed by the eye.

At the crest of his head was a golden gleam, a permanent mark that shone with the glory of the four rings upon his wings.

Pushing his change from his mind, Humphrey said, "I know how to save Esmeralda!" Running outside of the inn, Humphrey pulled his whistle from his pack, which now hung by his side like a messenger's bag, and pulled out the whistle that Adam had given him. He blew into it as hard as he could.

For a few moments all was silent; the sound of the ants massing near the town was even still in the wake of the whistle. Then...when Humphrey had given up hope on his idea, he heard a sound, louder than the ants, and far more dangerous. Creaking and thunderous, the sound grew nearer and nearer until he heard a familiar voice say, "I see you have decided to call in your favor, my friend!"

Adam, the crab, stood tall in front of a horde that came to the town, a glistening, ruby-studded crown upon his head, and said, "We are legion."

Stretching his wings for the first time, Humphrey leapt into the air and flew, so easy and fluid it could easily be believed he'd never crawled upon the ground at all and had flown his whole life. Flying high above the town, Humphrey saw that there were thousands upon thousands of crabs massed in growing camps behind the town.

Flying back down, he kept himself level with Adam, King of the Crabs and said, "You have not come for wealth...have you?"

Adam smiled darkly and said, "We have…other goals as well, but have no fear. You have saved my life, and I shall return the favor on this day."

Putting the concerning thoughts of crabs overwhelming the forest aside, Humphrey told the king of the events that had transpired since they'd met. Frowning in frustration, Adam said, "Then I have not only a chance to repay my debt, but also a fantastic opportunity to deal a blow to those who would have harmed me."

Looking to the distance, where the ants had raised a massive hill to their king's glory, Humphrey dug into his pack and found the stick he'd taken. He directed all of the inhabitants to the hill and said, "We will take back Esmeralda!"

Chapter Four

King Adam smiled and directed all of his forces to allow the various creatures of the town to ride upon them into battle. Raising their claws in response, a loud, vicious, hiss grew from the horde. Adam said, "Humphrey, my friend, we shall lay waste to these fools who would harm me!"

Flying forward ahead of the crabs and their riders, Humphrey flew to the first of many, many, many ant hill outposts. He struck it with his stick, and in that instant, a flash of lighting struck the hill, and his stick became a glowing, white sword.

Beautiful and thin, the sword had a ruby set within its hilt, but was pure white otherwise. As he flew from outpost to outpost ahead of his army, every hill he struck burst into white flames that sent his opponents flying, and filled his horde with morale to move forward.

Fighting the millions of ants that had come to attack them, his horde grew more emblazoned with every foe defeated. Soon Humphrey and his army stood before the largest hill. From the top of the hill, a massive tarantula climbed out, roaring at the world in rage, and atop it rode the ant king, Antemodes.

Within Antemodes' arms, bound and gagged, was Esmeralda, struggling at her bindings. Antemodes spoke: "HUMPHREY. You have defiled my name and harmed my people in our efforts to stop the crustacean menace from overwhelming the forest! In addition to this stupidity, you now assist them in their efforts to crush the only force capable of stopping them! How much more do you intend to trample on our pride as defenders of the forest?!"

Humphrey flew up to the king, with Adam in close pursuit, and spoke quietly, his voice full of rage, "Your soldiers were harming someone guilty of no crime! I did what any good-hearted being would do under the circumstances. You, however, have not only condoned their cruelty, but have now taken an innocent girl! You must be punished!"

In Antemodes' arms, Esmeralda stared, star-struck, at the new and glorious form that Humphrey had taken. Her eyes traced the lines of his wings and the new, lithe form of his body.

As Humphrey was speaking, the king released Esmeralda and drew his sword, swinging it at the butterfly. He swung as fast as lightning, but was stopped by some impenetrable force.

Humphrey, seeing his foe draw his blade, had reached into his pack for something to defend himself with. Out came a shield made of his silk, hardened and in the form of a large, round circle. King Adam, sneaking behind Antemodes during his attack on Humphrey, snatched Esmeralda from the king and shouted, "Humphrey! Now's the time!"

Striking forward with his shield, Humphrey attempted to hit Antemodes; but the tarantula leapt backwards to dodge the strike and as it fell, webs between its legs opened up like parachutes, and it glided to the ground. The king said, "Come, Humphrey, let us settle this!"

Chapter Five

Flying forward to meet the king in combat, Humphrey unfurled his wings and flew as fast as he could, his sword outstretched to meet his foe.

The tarantula leapt backwards again, his fangs bared in preparation for battle as Humphrey flew toward it. Antemodes, his sword flashing violently in the light, leapt forward off his mount and struck at Humphrey, missing by the barest inch.

Striking at the ant king, Humphrey used the force of his swing to send himself upward, only to see the king rapidly curl into a ball and stretch out. As he did so, a pair of wings unfurled with his outstretched body, and the king smiled darkly at Humphrey.

From the ground, Adam watched as the two fought, moving so fast they could barely be followed with the eye. Flitting from place to place, Humphrey and Antemodes' sword clashes were enunciated by blinding flashes of light, until finally they reached a stand-still, their blades moving at blinding speed around each other. As they fought in place, the air around them began to whip like storm winds. As their strikes grew stronger and stronger, finally Antemodes fell to the ground, clutching his blade arm in pain.

Slowly lowering himself to the ground, Humphrey said, "Do you want to end this now, Antemodes?"

His eyes flashing with hate, Antemodes' sword fell from his hand and he lunged at Humphrey in a rage. In a single fluid motion, Humphrey cut the ant king from shoulder to hip, bisecting him effortlessly.

All around them, the ants within the army fell to their knees, shocked at their king's demise. In their shock they were soon wiped to the last by the crabs and other creatures. The tarantula crawled forward and bowed humbly before Humphrey. It spoke, to Humphrey's surprise, in a low, gravelly voice. "I have always pledged my allegiance to the strongest. You are clearly the most deserving of this title, my lord."

Adam placed Esmeralda upon the tarantula and Humphrey asked, "What is your name, my friend."

The tarantula responded, "My name is Spook."

Humphrey nodded and said, "Spook, we have to leave. I'll fly myself…but you carry Esmeralda."

Nodding quietly, Spook said, "It shall be done."

Her body still reeling from the shock of the previous events, Esmeralda fell to the ravages of exhaustion and was soon sleeping.

Spook whispered quietly, "Where do we go, my lord?"

Humphrey looked out to the forest and said, "We go now to a place to rest and strengthen ourselves."

Chapter Six

Several weeks passed in Humphrey's search for the glade he'd found on his travels away from the castle. Adam, the blue crab king, had long since gone on ahead with a good portion of his army, to scout for remnants of Antemodes army. Keeping Esmeralda and himself alive with leaves he'd kept in his magical pack, Humphrey soon found what he sought, though something seemed different than the last time he'd been there. The glade, beautiful and green upon his last visit, was now a dark place, with dying plants, and almost no life to be seen. All around him, the very air seemed to drip with anger and darkness, almost physically oppressive in its power.

As he walked through, the rings on Humphrey's wings glowed brighter and brighter until they were the only source of light, shining like spotlights in the dim, dank locale. Esmeralda wrapped herself in a leaf from Humphrey's pack, only to find that it, too, had decayed, leaving only tatters of what had once been a healthy green leaf.

The deeper into the glade Humphrey went, the colder it got, until the only way he could function was to wrap his wings about him, keeping himself warm.

Spook walked slower, his master atop his back, and said, "Something isn't right here, master." Humphrey nodded and kept silent, wondering what had happened to this majestic place.

As Humphrey's group got closer to the center of the glade, there began a low sound, almost as though someone were in pain. Looking around curiously, Humphrey noticed something terrifying, though he couldn't put his finger on why it frightened him so.

The soft lights that had floated carelessly through the glade…were gone. Their light had been extinguished, and their warmth obliterated in the murk of the dark pall that had fallen over the glade.

When they reached a large, circular stone, Humphrey knew, though he would never hazard a guess how he'd known, that they'd found the center of the glade. Atop the stone, cracked and softly pulsating red, Humphrey noticed a slight glimmer.

Stepping off Spook, Humphrey walked forward and examined the glimmer, trying to figure out what it was. Touching his finger to it, he was shocked at his discovery. It was something that would mean nothing to anyone else. Stepping back, Humphrey whispered in horror, "Liquid Diamond."

As he finished his statement, the stone erupted into a massive vortex of furious red lights, each one angrier and darker than the last. Shielding himself from the light, closing his eyes, the stone began to leak sound as well, screeching like rough-hewn stone being pushed on stone. Louder and louder it grew until Humphrey felt his head might split from the sound.

Then…it stopped. As quickly as it had begun, the sound disappeared. Humphrey, on his knees clutching his head, was finally able to look around. In front of him were two eyes and a large mouth made of angry, red light. The eyes flickered for a bit, then large, black spots appeared, serving as irises, and the mouth opened and closed, as though testing its capabilities.

Humphrey stepped away from the lights and was immediately reprimanded. "I never gave you permission to move, Humphrey, King of the Butterflies."

The voice was low and dark, furious and calm, seething and neutral at the same time, somehow maintaining a perfect balance of hate and apathy with every word.

The voice spoke again, "The time has now come for you to pay for your crimes."

Chapter Seven

Humphrey's shock overtook his fear and he found himself yelling, "I have committed no crime!"

The voice spoke again, the power of its words physically pushing Humphrey backwards until he was forced up against Spook. "You have not only allowed an enemy of the forest to intrude here, you have also aided that intruder in the murder of my home's guardian!"

Humphrey stood confused for a moment and then said, "Antemodes…"

The voice spoke in a slow crescendo, climbing the scale of rage. "Antemodes was the guardian of the Glade of Awakening! It is here in this place that the life and strength of the forest is born and lives! It is here, in the Glade of Awakening, where kings, like yourself, are chosen. And lastly, it is here that the true magic of the forest resides! The sanctity of this place has been shattered, ruined well beyond repair, and it is YOU whom I hold responsible!"

Ignoring the statement about kings, Humphrey shouted back, "Antemodes attempted to murder me! He threatened a village of innocent people to strike me down in his personal vendetta! I have done nothing wrong! I don't even know what you are!"

The face condensed and shrunk until it was an elderly butterfly; its wings were as liquid silver, and its body seemed to be made of living ruby. Walking to Humphrey, the being said in a tired voice, "My name is Gaia, father of the forest. Antemodes told me of your heroic actions to save the blue crab, Adam. Though he spoke highly of your actions, he questioned your intent. You see…Adam, as king of the blue crabs, has begun his invasion of the forest. Finding this place solely by accident, Adam saw the Pool of Light and desired it, seeing it for its potential, instead of its true purpose."

Humphrey asked, "Pool of Light?"

Nodding his head forebodingly, Gaia spoke softly. "The pool of liquid diamond, as you and he so aptly described it, is used to choose true kings in times of need or danger. It manifests their good spirit and intentions as a physical capability to aid them in their travels. It also instills a sense of wonder and natural obedience in any and all who should view the new king. However…it is not sentient…it cannot defend itself from attack. As such, I have had Antemodes and his family watching over the Glade of Awakening for thousands of years. Adam came, seeking to steal that powerful tool, and was stopped in his tracks by Antemodes' men. When you stopped them, my friend assumed you an enemy and requested your trial. He never mentioned any personal motives to me…so I do apologize for my accusations."

Humphrey sat down and said, "What will happen now?"

Gaia sighed sadly and said, "There is a way to stop Adam and his army, though they will all be significantly stronger due to the Pool of Light that their king has stolen."

Humphrey jumped forward and said, "What way! Tell me!"

Gaia waved his arm at the ground before them, and it opened up to reveal a pool of what seemed to be liquid shadow. No reflection shone upon its surface. What little light there was seemed to be consumed by its depths.

"This is the Pool of Naught, Humphrey…it is the antithesis of the Pool of Light. In the Pool of Light's absence, it is this, the Pool of Naught, which has supplied its waters to the Glade of Awakening. This is why this realm is so touched by shadow now, why this once-beautiful glade is now steeped in shadow."

Humphrey asked, "If you're the father of the land, why can't you simply create another Pool of Light?"

Gaia frowned and said, "It is impossible. Duality is the one truth of this world we live in, Humphrey. For every light, there is an equally deep darkness. In the absence of the light, the darkness will step forward to take its place. Nobody can create something from nothing."

Humphrey nodded an assent and asked, "So, what do we do?"

Gaia looked toward Esmeralda and said, "You were to take that girl as a wife, correct?"

Humphrey nodded and Gaia spoke once more. "Duality is the truth, Humphrey." Looking at Humphrey he said, "For every light," he turned to look at Esmeralda, "there must be an equally deep darkness."

Walking toward Esmeralda, Gaia spoke softly. "The world is built from light, so easily manipulated and controlled…the heart and soul of living creatures, however, is built purely from darkness. It learns of light after its birth…but all hearts must learn that; none are born in it."

Taking Esmeralda in his arms, he brought her to the Pool of Naught and slowly lowered her into it, letting her float adrift.

Humphrey watched, confused, until Esmeralda began to sink into the pool and he yelled, "What are you doing!? She'll drown in there!"

Lunging forward to save her, Humphrey found he couldn't move an inch forward. Small vines had wrapped themselves around his legs, keeping him in place. As Esmeralda sank, Humphrey fell desperate and he said, "But she's so perfect…she can't die…"

All around them the glade went ominously silent and Gaia turned to Humphrey, waving his hand mysteriously.

"In order to reach any level of real power, a sacrifice must be made. Life is the sacrifice for power, Humphrey. It is a price even you have paid, many times over."

For a brief instant, Humphrey felt his wings burn, as though aflame. When the pain passed, he felt a rush of power surge through him, and suddenly he could see through the dark as though it were day.

"I have removed your limits, Humphrey. You have reached the highest level of power you can possibly achieve…I only hope it will be enough. My sister, Adaquare, has sent Adam to conquer this realm by any means possible…he has already done her bidding and made the ocean his…you do not have an easy trial ahead of you."

"Who is Adaquare?" Humphrey asked.

Gaia turned his glittering eyes upon Humphrey and said, "She is my sister…Mother of the Ocean, a jealous and vicious spirit who longs for all things she cannot have."

The Pool of Naught began to bubble and shake and Humphrey stepped back, fearful of what would emerge.

Chapter Eight

The pool exploded outward, a spiraling pillar of darkness erupting forth from the center of the pool. As the pillar spiraled, Humphrey felt the air grow cold and still, until finally he thought he saw the dark water freezing. This freezing continued until finally the pillar and all water around it was frozen solid and he asked, "What is this?"

"Warmth and fire are the sons of light, Humphrey. They, however, are easily engulfed by their cousins, the daughters of dark, cold and ice."

Stepping forward, Humphrey placed his hand on the pillar and large cracks began to form around it. As the ice began to shatter, Humphrey felt a pressure pushing back on his hand. As the ice fell away, he saw the glitter of soft, red eyes among the shards.

Two wings, completely black like liquid shadow, fluttered against his wings, now softly glowing white like liquid light. The red eyes moved closer to his. Feeling no fear, he moved closer to them and felt the caress of dainty arms wrap him in a tight embrace. Holding the source of his embracer, he heard a voice, like music dancing through flower petals say, "I am here."

Gaia stepped forward and the voice said, "Thank you, Gaia...I am ready to stand by my king now."

Humphrey looked again and saw an unfamiliar face, and asked who the person was. Draped in shadow, converted to near unfathomable beauty, was Esmeralda, who spoke softly, "I am your queen, my love, and we shall right these wrongs."

Gaia gently tapped their heads and said, "In the name of my creation, the forest, I dub thee, King Humphrey, Defender of Light, and Queen Esmeralda, Herald of Naught. May you save and rule all of my creation with a fair and noble hand."

Humphrey and Esmeralda closed their eyes and kissed each other, lovingly holding each other. When they opened their eyes they were no longer in the glade; they were surrounded by smoke and fire.

Looking around in confusion, they found that they were surrounded by a horde of butterflies and caterpillars, all armed to the teeth and prepared for war. The army began to cheer and Humphrey said, "I don't know how we got here….but let us end this."

Chapter Nine

Flying high into the air, Humphrey and Esmeralda both said in unison, "Go forth, and stop the crabs." Their army marched forward, weapons drawn, and were soon met by a similarly sized army of crabs.

The crabs, however, were larger than before. Their claws were easily twenty times the size of any caterpillar, and they glowed a soft shade of white. Gritting their teeth, Humphrey's army crashed forward into the horde, cutting and slashing through the hard-armored plates of the crabs. Seeing his army at work, Humphrey nodded and motioned for Esmeralda to follow him, and they flew toward the rear of the army.

He found Adam atop a large snake, watching the war and laughing at his foes. Approaching Adam, Humphrey yelled, "Adam! Stop this! There is no need for this madness!"

Adam turned to Humphrey and spoke quietly, his voice reverberating through Humphrey's mind. "I do this for the glory of Adaquare! I do this for power! I do this, so that we may have what belongs to us!"

Humphrey flew to his former friend and asked, "What do we have that is yours?"

Adam swung his claw at Humphrey and said angrily, "EVERYTHING IS OURS! This world will fall to my army, and all shall belong to me!"

Catching Adam's claw in a single hand, Humphrey said sadly, "If you will not listen to reason…you leave me one choice, my friend."

Opening his free hand, Humphrey concentrated. All around him, the world grew darker. The light around them faded, and reformed in the palm of Humphrey's hand. He closed it, creating a blazing sword of light. Calmly, Humphrey targeted the king's weak spot, between his armored plates, and jabbed his sword at the point. Adam smiled and said, "You are not the only one with the power of light, my friend." A soft white field of light stopped Humphrey's sword in place, keeping him from moving any farther forward.

Opening his claw, still pointed at Humphrey's face, light began to focus within. Sensing the growing power, Humphrey released the claw and leapt backwards just as a massive beam of light erupted from within it, blazing a path of destruction that killed Adam's guardians, leaving nothing but ash in its wake.

Watching his enemy warily, Humphrey felt a rush of cold air fly past him and saw Esmeralda grab Adam's claw. He felt the temperature of the air drop rapidly. Adam screamed loudly in pain and Esmeralda said, "How dare you try to harm my husband!" Humphrey watched as a thick layer of ice grew over Adam's claw, and Esmeralda twisted her wrist slightly, causing the claw to snap off at the base.

Leaping backward, Esmeralda snapped her fingers, and long spears of ice appeared around Adam, floating softly in the air. Humphrey touched her shoulder and said, "This is too much, my love…he has made bad choices…but we cannot kill him."

Esmeralda turned and kissed Humphrey gently and said, "My love…nothing else will stop this…he has committed a grave crime…and he will return stronger if we don't. Look, already his stolen power restores him to full health."

Looking at Adam, Humphrey's spirits fell when he saw the crab's claw rapidly regenerating, and laughter forming on his face. Turning away, Humphrey nodded, and Esmeralda lifted her arm and motioned her hand downward. The spears of ice struck downward. Hearing the sound of ice colliding with the snake's head, Humphrey assumed his friend dead, the battle over.

Beginning to fly away he heard an angry voice, "I AM MORE THAN YOU! YOU CANNOT STOP MY INVASION. YOU CANNOT HOLD US DOWN. WE SHALL ARISE."

Looking back, confused, Humphrey saw beams of bright, powerful light streaking toward Adam. He saw that the army of crabs were shrinking, their glow disappearing, as Adam grew brighter and stronger and larger. He grew so large and heavy that the snake that was carrying him was crushed beneath his weight.

Faced with this enormous enemy, Humphrey and Esmeralda both released a collective sigh and flew vertically until they were level with Adam's eyes. Humphrey said, "You still have a chance, my friend…this can end here, and we can all come out of this alive."

Adam's response was to aim his claw at Humphrey and release a blast of energy so large that it was as thick as a tree. Humphrey felt the air around him begin to burn with its power. Looking down in sadness, he lifted a hand and stopped the blast in its path. The beam's power flowed into him and increased his power, making his wings glow with fierce light.

In the moments after the blast, the area was left in near-perfect darkness. Humphrey felt Esmeralda drawing from its power, getting stronger and stronger, until her wings seemed to be absorbing the light around them.

Adam screamed in rage, "WHY CAN'T I KILL YOU? WHAT MAKES YOU SO POWERFUL!?"

"We are the rightful bearers of the power you have tried to steal. You can't stop light with light."

Chapter Ten

Humphrey and Esmeralda took each other's hand and pointed the opposite hand at Adam and said together, "You must be stopped." Humphrey added quietly, "My friend."

Simultaneously they released blasts of energy, light and dark that fed off of each other and made the other stronger, at a singular point in front of Adam. When they collided, they created an explosion of air that both drained Adam of his power and began to do more and more damage to him. In the last moments of the blast, Adam shrank back to his normal size, and his army turned to Humphrey and dropped their weapons, bowing in fear and respect.

Humphrey flew to Adam and said, "I don't care what your mistress has requested of you, my friend. This place is my home, and I will defend it as best I can."

Adam looked at Humphrey and said, "You still call me friend...why?"

Humphrey smiled and said, "Nobody is perfect, my friend...you did what you thought was best for your people...I would do the same in your position. You are my friend because despite your missteps, you only did what you genuinely believed was best. There was no personal assault made here...damage can be healed, lives can be mended...though I do not think you will be able to walk freely...I will permit you to stay with me, so long as you wish it."

Adam looked at Humphrey briefly, and for a moment, Humphrey thought Adam would deny his offer. But he was happily surprised to hear the crab say to a nearby aide, "Tell the army they are to return to the ocean…tell Adaquare that there will be no further invasions."

His aide nodded and touched Humphrey's shoulder and said, "I don't know how you did it…but since he spoke with the Ocean Spirit, he has been obsessed with this madness. I'm sorry for the trouble we've caused."

Humphrey stopped the aide and said, "What do you know of the Ocean Spirit?"

The crab responded, "Only that she is a dangerous and angry being…and that she cannot leave her cave. She called my king to her when he was nearby one day, and he remained there for over a week, speaking and consulting with her."

Letting the crab go, Humphrey turned to Adam and asked, "How do you feel?"

Adam responded softly, "Ashamed. I don't know why…but I can't even remember my original reason for this invasion…so much of this is a blur as of late…the only thing I remember clearly is you saving my life in the glade…I'm so sorry, my friend."

Humphrey thought on this for a moment and turned to Esmeralda and said, "Come, my love…we're going to the glade."

"We're taking him with us?" Esmeralda asked incredulously. Nodding, Humphrey said, "I have an idea."

Humphrey bid farewell to his army. Colwin, the commander was a butterfly of massive size, with green and brown wings resembling camouflage. Humphrey asked Colwin to inform his parents he'd be returning soon. Bowing at the waist, Colwin spoke an affirmative, and began gathering his army and leading them back to the castle.

Humphrey and Esmeralda set out, with Adam in tow. A week later, they found the Glade of Awakening.

Chapter Eleven

Walking into the glade, Humphrey was happy to see that it was even more beautiful now than it had been the first time he'd entered. Now, rather than being the embodiment of light or shadow, it was a beautiful place in perfect balance within itself.

Gaia descended from the air, his wings immobile, and said, "You have brought their king to me?"

Humphrey nodded and said, "Gaia…it is my opinion that Adam did not do the things he's done under his own volition…I believe that he was being controlled, to a small extent, and I believe we should give him a chance to prove his true intentions."

Gaia turned to where the Pool of Light had been and saw that it was filled with light again. He thought for a moment.

Speaking slowly and thoughtfully, Gaia said, "Light, when stolen…can't be stolen back…it must be returned of the thief's own volition. The fact that you were able to return the light here tells me that somewhere in Adam's heart, he did not want this war, or the power he possessed. What is your suggestion, Humphrey?"

Humphrey nodded at Esmeralda, and she waved her hand over the earth. A ring of dark power began to grow, until it was just larger than Adam.

Humphrey began to speak. "I've learned something of light and darkness in the war…and in the time we've traveled here. Darkness has the power to harness ideas and dreams…light has the power to force them into reality. Used separately, they reject each other. Used together, they grow from each other, and accomplish things that would never be possible otherwise."

Waving his hand over the ring of darkness, Humphrey channeled light into it. After a moment, the ring was soon a portal of seawater, and Gaia said, "What are you doing, Humphrey?"

"Giving my friend a chance to be the king he truly is."

Gaia looked at Humphrey curiously for a moment. Humphrey said, "I would like Adam to take the place of Antemodes as the protector of the glade. This portal will allow him to not only watch over his home, but to keep watch over anything that would attack our home."

"This is a very dangerous idea," Gaia said.

"I was skeptical at first as well," Esmeralda said, and continued, "but Humphrey told me something that changed my mind."

Gaia asked, "What was that?"

Esmeralda said, smiling, "The moment the power of light was removed from him, Adam made no attempt to take the power back; he lost all menace. It was as though he had been cleansed. Once clean, his mind was clear to think properly. I believe, as Humphrey does, that your sister did something to Adam to make him more aggressive, more war-loving."

Humphrey stepped forward and touched Gaia as he said, "If Adam or the crabs should ever try to harm this place again, I will wipe them out myself, with no mercy. I doubt, though, that this will be the case."

Gaia thought for a moment and addressed the crab king. "You understand this situation…correct?"

Adam bowed deeply and said, "I merely wish to make amends for what I've done."

Gaia asked cynically, "Do you believe that you were changed by my sister?"

Adam made a quiet sound and said, "In my opinion, it is irrelevant whether I was altered or not. I have still committed a terrible crime against a friend. I believe that Humphrey's answer will allow me to not only show repentance for my crimes against the forest…but also to take the place of King Antemodes, who I helped to destroy. It will fix the problem of this place lacking a defender, and stop others from trying what I tried."

"A good answer…sincere…and you seem likeable enough… I'll allow it, Humphrey," Gaia said, as he turned to Humphrey.

Humphrey bowed slightly and said to Esmeralda, "Start the other portal, my love."

Gaia sensed the gist of Humphrey's second idea and said, "A portal directly here will certainly help with many things, young one."

Humphrey said, "We may have saved the forest, but we don't necessarily know what's best for it. A portal here will allow us to consult you for major decisions or problems. It will also allow us to return our power before our death. Adam's attack will have emboldened others who would assault our home or us ourselves. A way to get here can be closed quickly enough to stop them from endangering the glade itself."

Gaia nodded and said, "If my first sister has been so emblazoned as to attack this place, I'm certain that my youngest sister will follow suit someday soon. I approve of the second portal as well, my friend."

Humphrey directed his hand at the portal of darkness his wife had made and channeled light into it, opening a portal into a room he'd remembered to be empty within the castle he'd grown up in.

Walking to it, he turned to Gaia and said, "Thank you." Gaia nodded, and as Humphrey walked through he heard Adam diving into the ocean portal to gather his fellow crabs to defend the glade.

Chapter Twelve

Expecting to walk into an empty room, Humphrey was met with fanfare, and a room filled with beauty. His parents flew to him and held him close. His father said, "Colwin flew to us as fast as his wings could carry him, and told us all that has happened. We have missed you so very much, my child."

Humphrey held his parents close to him and said, "I have missed you all as well. I'm sorry for my foolishness."
Shaking their heads, the queen spoke happily, "All that matters is that our son is finally home! Not only this, but he brings the most beautiful butterfly to be his wife!"

Laughing happily with his parents, Humphrey looked around for his brothers and saw them in front of the crowd, all butterflies with glorious wings, looking down at the floor. Walking to them silently, unsure what to expect, his eldest brother grabbed him and held him. Humphrey felt water hit his shoulder where his brother's head rested, and realized his brothers were crying.

His eldest brother spoke, his voice choked with tears. "I'm so very sorry, Humphrey. We have been horrible…we cast you out…we denied you the love you deserved. We understand if you hate us."

Humphrey pulled away from his brother and said, "How could I possibly hate you? Any of you? You're my brothers, and I love you all. What happened is behind us, and all that matters is what we do now."

A smile grew on all his brothers' faces and they tackled him, happily hugging him, and asking him questions about his journey prior to the war with the crabs.

He pulled away one last time and reached into his bag, wanting to have them taste the leaves from the glade. He was shocked to find that the rings that had been disappearing from his body since he first left the glade had appeared in his bag, shrunken to hand size, and glowing fiercely. Calling his brothers over, he gave them all a ring and said, "There is much work to do, but when the time comes, I am to be king. I want nothing more than to have you, my brothers, by my side. Take these and be my stewards, my closest friends and confidants."

Expecting argument about his claim to kingship, he was happily surprised when they all put the rings on and dropped to a knee, vowing their allegiance to his sovereignty.

As his brothers fell to their knees, all the other caterpillars and butterflies in the room fell to their knees behind them, and vowed their allegiance to him. Turning to his parents, his father said, "We knew you were destined for great things, my child. You have done so much, and you will do so much more. Tonight there will be a celebration the likes of which has never been seen!"

Walking to him, Esmeralda held Humphrey close to her and said, "We have our home, my love."
Humphrey nodded and said, "The road ahead will be difficult…but we are not alone…we are never alone."

And so, with his friends the crabs defending the Glade of Awakening and his family at his side, Humphrey and Esmeralda looked to the challenges ahead with their heads held high.

*Coming soon. Watch for another exciting Humphrey Adventure.

**Copyrighted by Julie Parker